GOODBYE OLD YEAR, HELLO NEW YEAR

by Frank Modell

Greenwillow Books
New York

FIRST EDITION
1   2   3   4   5   6   7   8   9   10

Library of Congress Cataloging in Publication Data

Modell, Frank.
Goodbye old year, hello new year.
Summary: Marvin and Milton want to
celebrate the coming of the new year
but fall asleep before midnight.
[1. New Year—Fiction]   I. Title.
II. Title: Goodbye old year, hello new year.
PZ7.M714Go   1984   [E]   84-4020
ISBN 0-688-03938-3
ISBN 0-688-03939-1 (lib. bdg.)

TO FLICKER

Marvin and Milton liked celebrations—
and New Year's was the first celebration
of the year.

"I know what I'd like to do,"
said Marvin. "I'd like to go
way up in a spaceship and say,
'Happy New Year, everybody!'"

"That's silly," said Milton.
"Spaceships don't do skywriting."

"I bet if we make a lot of noise
   and shout Happy New Year right out
   our window, lots of people will
   hear us," said Marvin.

"The new year comes at midnight.
    We can't stay up that late,"
  said Milton.

"We don't have to stay up," said Marvin.
"Before we go to sleep, we set our
    alarm clocks for midnight. We can
    have a big celebration."
"I better go look for my alarm clock,
    if we're going to do that," said Milton.

"First we have to get things ready
so we'll be ready as soon as the
alarm goes off," said Marvin.
"What things?" said Milton.
"Balloons, pots, pans, funny hats,"
said Marvin.

"I'm ready," said Marvin.

"Terrific," said Milton.
"See you at midnight."

While Marvin and Milton slept,

everyone else was up celebrating.

"I think we missed it," said Marvin.
"My alarm clock didn't go off."

"I didn't hear mine," said Milton.

"I guess it's too late to celebrate now,"
said Milton.

"No, it isn't," said Marvin. "The day
doesn't really start till the sun
comes up."

"It'll be up pretty soon," said Milton.
"We better not waste time."

"Get ready. Here it comes," said Marvin.

"There goes the old year," said Milton.

FOR
HOORAY
HOO RAY
FOR THE NEW
HAPP
HAPPY NOOOOO
HOO RAY
BANG
IT'S NEW YEARS
RAY
BANG
BANG
HOORAY, IT'S NEW YEARS
CLANG
CLANG
CLANG
CLANK

"I think we celebrated enough for this year," said Marvin.

"What do we do now?" said Milton.
"Now it's refreshment time," said Marvin.
"What refreshments?" asked Milton.
"You'll see," said Marvin.

"Happy New Year, Milton."

"Happy New Year, Marvin."